The Worst Wizard

Also by John McLay and Martin Brown:
The Dragon's Dentist

There are lots of Early Reader stories
you might enjoy.

Look at the back of the book or,
for a complete list, visit
www.orionbooks.co.uk

The Worst Wizard

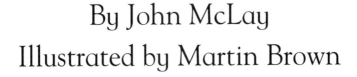

By John McLay

Illustrated by Martin Brown

Orion
Children's Books

First published in Great Britain in 2015
by Orion Children's Books
a division of the Orion Publishing Group Ltd
Orion House
5 Upper Saint Martin's Lane
London WC2H 9EA
An Hachette UK Company

1 3 5 7 9 10 8 6 4 2

The Orion Publishing Group's policy is to use papers that are natural,
renewable and recyclable products and made from wood grown in
sustainable forests. The logging and manufacturing processes are expected
to conform to the environmental regulations of the country of origin.

ISBN 978 1 4440 1290 3

A catalogue record for this book
is available from the British Library.

Printed and bound in China

www.orionbooks.co.uk

To the Morris family – J.M.
To my niece, Emma Chisholm – M.B.

Contents

Chapter One

Harry was a knight-in-waiting. His name was top of the list to become the next knight.

His family were all knights.
Large ones.

Harry was a shield cleaner.
A small one.

"Are you OK down there, Harry?" his sister would say when she walked past him. This was very annoying.

Harry's mother was always ruffling his hair. This was also very annoying.

Harry's best friend was a horse
called Oats. Oats had no problem
getting bigger.

Harry didn't get any bigger no
matter how much he ate.

"I need to be taller!" said Harry.

Chapter Two

One morning, Harry and Oats were in the courtyard when an idea struck Harry.

It wasn't an idea that popped
into his head. It was a hat that
somebody had thrown over the
castle wall.

Harry picked the hat up and
looked at it closely.

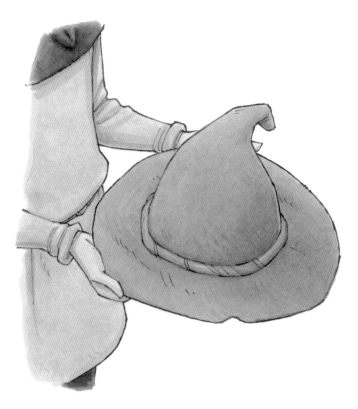

It was a bit like a wizard's hat.

"That's it!" he said to Oats. "I'll go and see Hocus Pocus! He'll be able to help me."

Hocus Pocus the moody Magician
who hated small boys and fat
horses?

No.

Hocus Pocus the sad Sorcerer who made everyone unhappy?

No.

Surely not Hocus Pocus the
wonky wizard who didn't know
one end of a spell from the other?

Yes. That Hocus Pocus.
Hocus Pocus the Wizard.

"Hocus Pocus will make me taller," said Harry. "He can do some magic. I'll need to be a lot bigger when I become a knight. Which could be any day."

Harry rushed off to pack his bag
for the journey.
Oats began munching on the hat.

Chapter Three

Harry and Oats left the castle and set off to find Hocus Pocus the Wizard.

Tucked into
his belt was
his special
dragon tooth
sword.

In his bag were
lots of oats in
case Oats got
peckish.

On his head was
his dented old
helmet.

At the last minute, Harry had decided to borrow his sister's shield. Hocus Pocus might throw a spell at him.

It started to rain.

Harry did not like getting wet.

Nor did Oats.

They soon came across a man
under a tree. "Are you Hocus
Pocus?" said Harry.
The man laughed. "No! I'm
Eric. Why do you want that
weird wizard?"

"I need to be taller," said Harry.
"So my dad will make me a
knight."
"Well, I'd steer clear of Hocus
Pocus if I were you. He's useless."
"Really?" said Harry.

"I went to Wizard School with him," said the man. "He'll turn you into a cabbage if you're not careful. He once turned my foot into a carrot."

Oats and Harry looked at each other and gulped.

Chapter Four

"Can you tell me the way to his house?" asked Harry.

The man pointed. "Take the path through the Great Forest. Hocus Pocus lives in the middle. Don't say I didn't warn you!"

Harry and Oats soon found
a strange looking cottage.
Something about it wasn't
quite right.

"Anybody there?" said Harry.
"Mr Hocus Pocus? Hello?"

Suddenly, a bolt of blue magic
shot out of the door.
It hit Oats in the face.

Oats turned into…

…a donkey.

"Oats!" said Harry.

Chapter Five

"Sorry about that," said an odd man in a big shiny helmet. It was Hocus Pocus the Wizard!

"Eee-Haw!" cried Oats.

"I wasn't expecting visitors."
Hocus Pocus shuffled back inside.

"Please turn him back into a
horse!" said Harry.
The wizard shook his head.
"I wish I could."

Harry picked up a book and opened it. He pointed at a spell. "What about this one?"
Hocus Pocus scratched his chin. "No, no, no, no. That looks much too hard."

"I could try," said Harry.
The wizard chuckled. "You? It
takes hundreds of years to train
as a wizard."
"Eee-Haw!" cried Oats.

Harry picked up a wand and
stumbled through the spell.
Badly.

There was a flash
of blue smoke and
the big red chair
turned into a
golden harp.

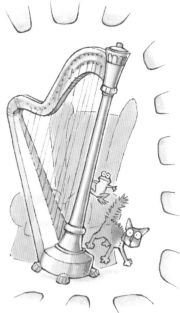

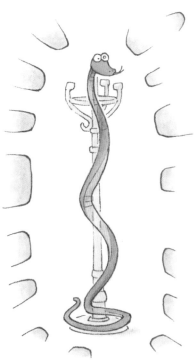

Harry waved
his wand madly.
The hat stand
turned into
a snake and
slithered away.

"Stop! Stop!" said Hocus Pocus.
"You're worse than I am!"

"What am I going to do?" said
Harry. Harry and Hocus Pocus
looked at Oats. "It's no use. He's
never going to change back."

Oats the donkey fainted.

Chapter Six

Harry sat in the nearest chair,
then hopped up again.

"Sorry. Are these yours?" he asked,
holding up a pair of glasses.
"My glasses!" cried the wizard.
"I haven't seen those for years."

"But how do you read the spell books?" asked Harry.
"Not very well. That's why I am such a rubbish wizard."

Harry was excited. "Now you can turn Oats back into a horse!"
"Yes, I can," said Hocus Pocus.
He read a big, tricky spell.
There was a bolt of blue magic.
Oats was a horse again!

"Thank you," said Harry.
"No, thank you for finding my glasses!" The wizard looked around. "What can I give you as a reward?"

"Can you make me taller?"
Hocus Pocus chuckled.
"Sorry, no. Even with glasses
I'm not that good."
Then Harry looked at his flashy
helmet and smiled.

Back at the castle, Harry sat cleaning the shields. He wasn't any taller, but he had a brand new helmet.

"Nice head gear," said his brother. Harry's sister looked around the barn. "Have you seen my shield, squirt? I can't find it anywhere."

Harry and Oats ran to hide.

What are you going to read next?

Have more adventures with Horrid Henry,

or save the day with Anthony Ant!

Become a superhero with Monstar,

float off to sea with Algy,

or have your very own Pirates' Picnic.

Grow carrots with Lottie and Dottie,

make magic with The Witch Dog,

and cast a spell with The Three Little Magicians.

Enjoy all the Early Readers.